For Dimitri – J.W.
For Mum – H.B.

This paperback edition first published in 2020
by Andersen Press Ltd.
First published in Great Britain in 2019
by Andersen Press Ltd.,
20 Vauxhall Bridge Road, London SW1V 2SA.
Text copyright © Jeanne Willis, 2019.
Illustration copyright © Hrefna Bragadottir, 2019.

The rights of Jeanne Willis and
Hrefna Bragadottir to be identified as the
author and illustrator of this work have been
asserted by them in accordance with the
Copyright, Designs and Patents Act, 1988.
All rights reserved.

1 3 5 7 9 10 8 6 4 2

Printed and bound in China.
British Library Cataloguing in
Publication Data available.
ISBN 978 1 78344 885 2

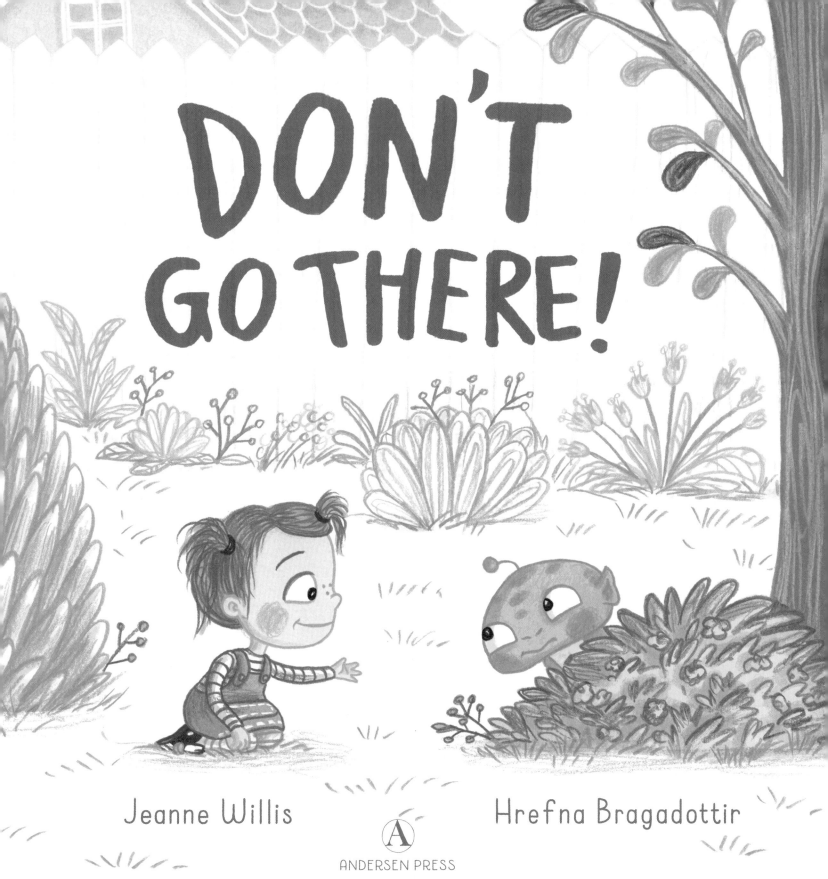

# DON'T GO THERE!

Jeanne Willis

Hrefna Bragadottir

ANDERSEN PRESS

I found a baby
Martian, he was
soft and small
and green.

He had the
sweetest little
face that I have
ever seen.

I kept him in my
room, which was a
silly thing to do,
because no one
had taught him...

# ...how to use the Loo!

They must have different toilets
where he lives in outer space.
I think that's why he always did it...

in the "Wrong" place!

I took him to
the bathroom
and I showed him
where to go.

But when he saw
the toilet, he yelled,

NO! NO!
NO!

"Too cold and hard and deep!" he cried.
"Too weird and wet for me!"

And he ran off down the stairs
to find another place to wee.

He emptied out the toy box
and he found my cowboy hat.

He turned it upside down
and then he tried to go in that.

It was far too soft and bendy,
as he sat upon the brim...

he fell inside
as it gave way
and crumpled
under him!

Still desperate to go, he perched
upon the litter bin.
But it was very chilly and
uncomfortable and thin.

He sat and he stood up again
but then what did he find...

... the litter bin was sticking to his little green behind!
I pulled and tugged, and finally it came off with a PLOP!

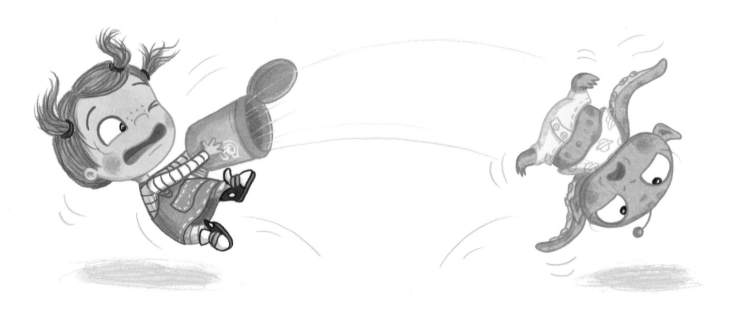

Then off he ran to find another place to park and stop.

He squatted on our goldfish bowl, I said:

# DON'T GO THERE!
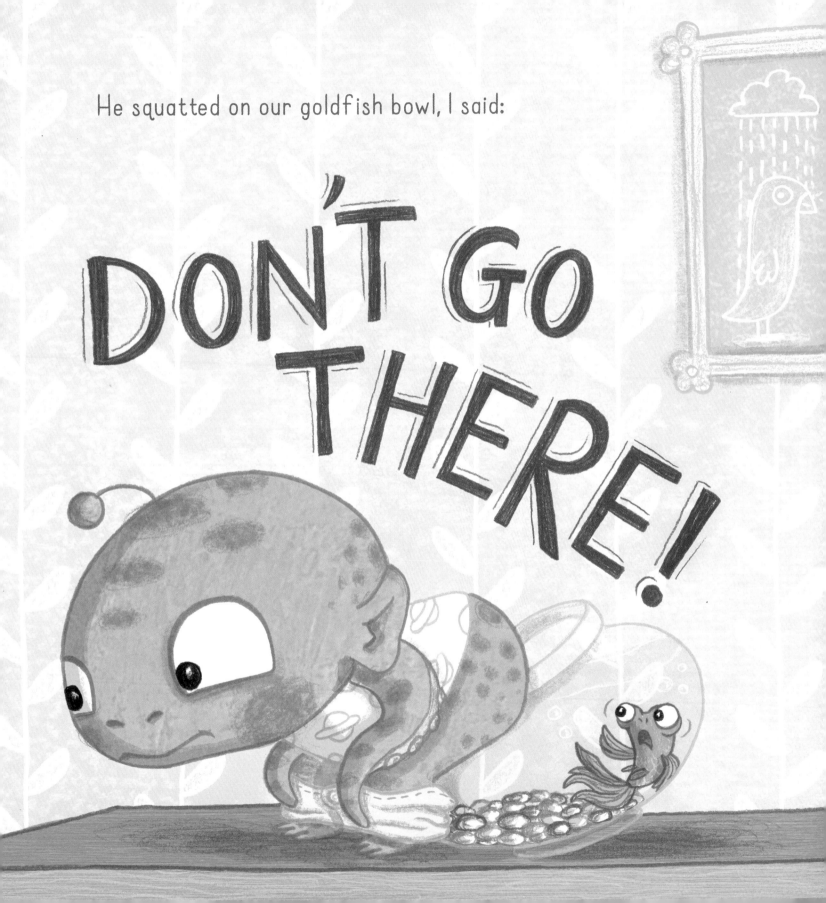

But,

*tinkle tinkle*

SPLASH CRASH

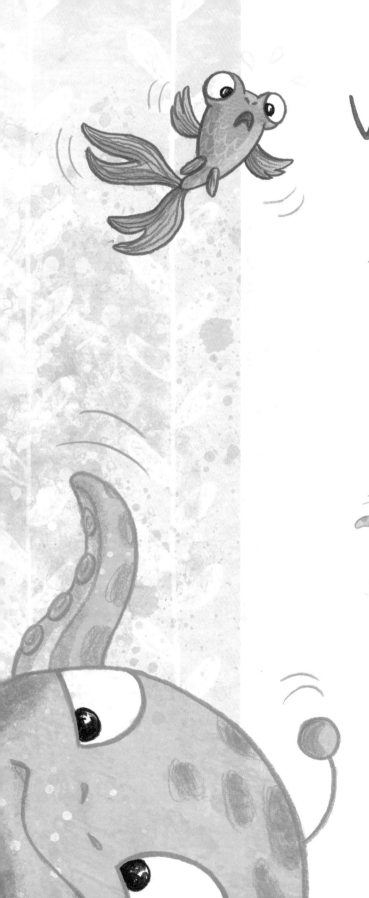

# Water everywhere!

I took him by the tentacle
and marched him to the loo.
There was only one thing for it:
I must show him what to do.

I sat down on the toilet seat
and sang The Toilet Song,
to teach him how to do it
so he wouldn't get it wrong.

Lid up,

Pants down,

bottom on the seat.

Sit still,
just chill,
till the job's
complete.

He listened and he watched and he seemed quite keen to go and do his business where I'd just been.

He didn't get it
quite right
(he's a Martian
to be fair).
He went...

Lid down, pants up, bottom in the air!

he flushed his <u>pants</u>!

But practice makes you perfect, so before very long,
he learned to perform The Toilet Song.
He knows where to go and what to do.

If he can use the lavatory, you can too!

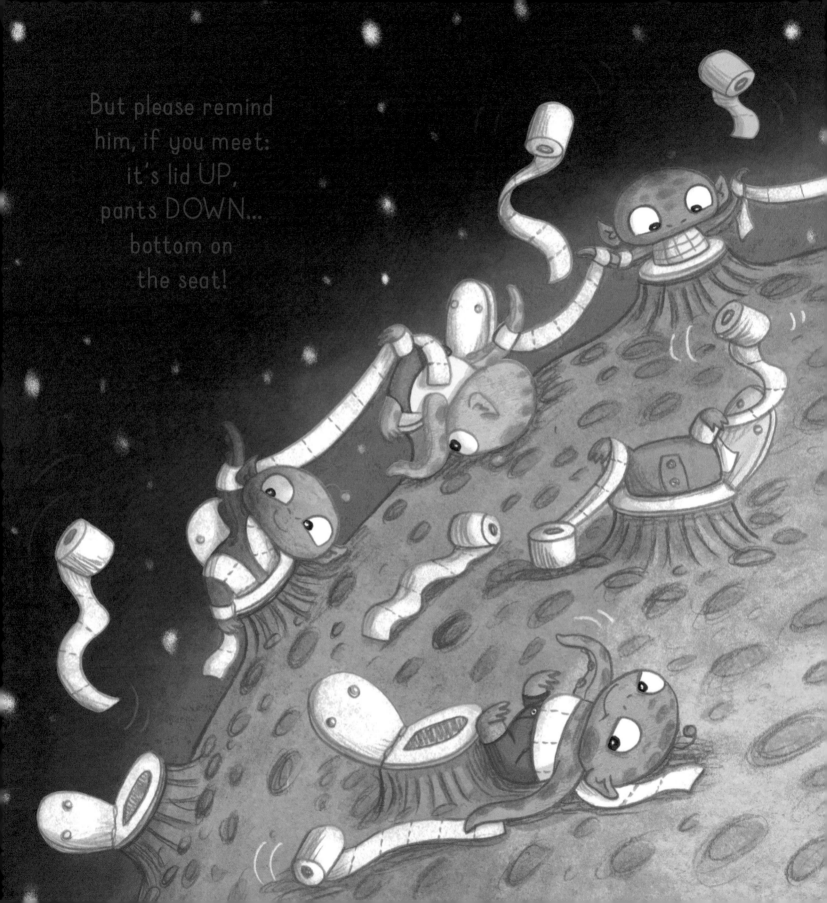

But please remind
him, if you meet:
it's lid UP,
pants DOWN...
bottom on
the seat!

# More books by Jeanne Willis to enjoy:

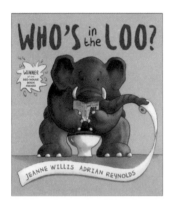

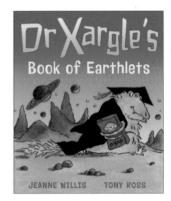

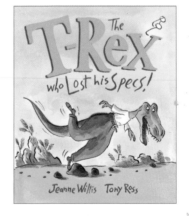